DATE DUE			

11036

F
AIE

Aiello, Barbara.

On with the show!

On With The Show!

Meet
BRENDA

Birthday: February 19
Best friends:
    Melody James
    Mark Riley
    Jennifer Hauser
    Leslie Rosenbaum
Hobbies:
    Listening to music
    Walking my dog Muffy
      ("Or does she walk me?")
Sports:
    Ping-Pong (with my Mom)
    Bike Riding (with my Dad)
Favorite food (Yum!):
    Mushroom pizza
    Baked potatoes with cheese
    Cocoa
      ("With extra marshmallows")
Favorite Subjects:
    Music
    Spelling
      ("I was the fourth-grade champ.")
Yuck!:
    Cleaning up *two* bedrooms
    Anchovies on my mushroom pizza

Brenda Dubrowski

THE KIDS ON THE BLOCK BOOK SERIES

On With The Show!

Featuring Brenda Dubrowski

Barbara Aiello and Jeffrey Shulman
Illustrated by Loel Barr

TWENTY-FIRST CENTURY BOOKS
FREDERICK, MARYLAND

Twenty-First Century Books
38 South Market Street
Frederick, Maryland 21701

Special Sales:

The Kids on the Block Book
Series is available at quantity dis-
counts with bulk purchase for
educational, charitable, business,
or sales promotional use. For in-
formation, please write to:
Marketing Director, Twenty-First
Century Books, 38 South Market
Street, Frederick, Maryland,
21701.

Printed in the United States of
America

9 8 7 6 5 4 3 2 1

Song Credits:

Composition: "My Girl"
Writers: William Robinson/
  Ronald White
Publisher: Jobete Music Co., Inc.
Copyright: December 1964

Composition: "The Twist"
Writer: Hank Ballard
Publisher: Hudson Bay Music, Inc.
Copyright: 1959 by Fort Knox
  Music, Inc. and Trio Music Co.,
  Inc. Copyright renewed.
All rights administered by Hud-
  son Bay Music, Inc.

Composition: "Mister Ed"
Writers: Jay Livingston/
  Ray Evans
Publishers: Jay Livingston Music/
  St. Angelo Music
Copyright: Renewed, 1988.

Library of Congress Cataloging-in-Publication Data
Aiello, Barbara
     On with the show!: featuring Brenda Dubrowski / by Barbara Aiello
and Jeffrey Shulman; illustrated by Loel Barr.
     (The Kids on the Block book series)
     Summary: A fifth-grader having trouble coming to grips with her
parents' divorce directs a class show of music from "The Good Old Days."
Includes a section of questions and answers about divorce.
     ISBN 0-941477-06-1
     [1. Divorce — Fiction.] I. Shulman, Jeffrey, 1951—   . II. Barr, Loel, ill.
III. Title. IV. Series: Aiello, Barbara. Kids on the Block book series.
PZ7.A269240n   1989   89-5008
[Fic]

To the children who teach us about differences—
and similarities

Dear Reader:

Who are The Kids on the Block? They are kids like
you. They like to do the same things you do. They share
your hopes and fears. And like you, they have differences.
You'll meet kids who are blind or have cerebral palsy. You'll
meet kids who are deaf or have asthma. And you'll meet
kids whose lives have been changed by divorce or drugs.

In The Kids on the Block Book Series, you'll find their
stories. You'll read stories about friendship and growing
up, stories about changes and challenges. But you won't
read about kids who are dependent, and you won't read
about superheroes, either. The Kids on the Block are
regular kids leading regular lives.

"I'm not an epileptic," one kid says. "I'm a person with
epilepsy." And that is the point. These kids are people:
different in the same ways that we are all different, alike
in the same ways that we are all alike.

We hope you enjoy their stories.

Barbara Aiello
Jeffrey Shulman

CHAPTER 1

"Brenda," Lisa said to me, "you're awfully quiet today, aren't you?"

"I guess I just don't have a lot to say," I mumbled back. Lisa let the silence work for a while. She was good at that. She said you could hear a lot in silence, if you knew how to listen for it.

Lisa Bell was my counselor. I started seeing her when my parents separated. I wasn't quite sure what was supposed to happen (I was afraid to go at first), but, now, it's nice just to have someone else to talk to. Someone who would listen . . . you know, listen to me.

I remember the first time I saw Lisa. It hurt so much to talk about what was going on, I was afraid I might cry. And I didn't want to do that. Not any more.

"Then, let's not talk about the divorce," she said.

I was surprised. "What else is as big as that?" I asked.

Lisa laughed a little laugh. "Oh, I imagine there are lots of things," she answered. There were, too. We talked about school. We talked about my friends. We talked about growing up. (It's a lot harder than I thought.) We talked about how things change. And how people change.

I wasn't sure why I kept on seeing Lisa. Maybe because she was easy to talk to, and these days, that counted for something. These days, it counted for a lot. And, somehow, we also talked about the divorce. It wasn't that Lisa asked me about it. It was just that my thoughts always seemed to end up there.

Lisa helped me really learn about divorce: how it's not my fault; how it's not the end of the world, or even the end of our family. I know that in their own way my parents still love each other. I know they both still love me. I know all those things.

The problem is, I don't always *feel* all those things. I don't always feel that way at all.

"Feelings have a life of their own," Lisa explained.

"You make it sound like feelings are real," I said.

"They're as real as can be," Lisa said seriously. "When they get hurt, they get *really* hurt. And they can stay hurt for a long, long time."

I was quiet today, but I guess the silence worked after all. "It's all the other kids," I finally said.

"The other kids at school?" Lisa asked.

"Yes," I said. "They just won't cooperate with me. I don't understand it. You know, the fifth-grade music show I told you about"—

"You're the director, aren't you?"

"I *was* the director, you mean." Lisa waited for an explanation. (She knows when to wait. That's one of the things I like about her.) "I've had it," I said.

"Do you want to tell me why?" she asked. (Lisa also knows when *not* to wait. That's another one of the things I like about her.) "Brenda?"

"I told you, it's the other kids. Ever since I was picked to be director of the show, they just won't listen to me. I didn't ask to be the director, you know. But a director has to . . . has to . . . well, a director has to direct, doesn't she? How can I direct if no one will listen to me?"

8

"Yes, that does sound like a problem," Lisa said. "Maybe you should tell me a little more about the music show. Why don't we start at the beginning?"

"It's a long story," I said.

"Brenda," Lisa replied, "that's the kind of story I like best."

"Okay," I said with a shrug. I took a deep breath and began: "I remember the first time I heard about the winter musical. It was a cold Friday afternoon."

CHAPTER 2

It was a cold Friday afternoon.

"Hey, Mom," I shouted when I saw my mother standing by the elevator of our apartment building. "You're home early." I usually got home from school before my Mom got home from work. That's because Mom was working more now that she and Dad were no longer married. Once in a while, though, Mom was there before me, and those times—well, it's hard to describe, but it was just one of the nicest feelings in the world.

"There was no heat in our office," Mom explained. She didn't really have to: she looked frozen. She was rubbing her hands together, and she had her ski hat squashed down all over her curly blond hair. "January," she said, like the words left a bad taste in her mouth. "It's a nasty month. What a way to start the weekend! What a way to start the year! Say, let's go make some hot cocoa."

"With or without?" I asked.

"On a day like today?" she said. "With extra marshmallows."

That was all right with me. Maybe January wasn't so bad after all. We took the elevator to the seventh floor ("Our lucky floor," Mom called it) and walked to our apartment. Our apartment: that was another change. When my parents separated, we sold our house, and Mom and I moved to the Woodburn Garden Apartments. Dad has an apartment, too, on the other side of town. "Now, aren't two apartments better than one house?" Mom and Dad used to ask, trying to cheer me up. I used to give them a look that just said "No."

While Mom took care of the cocoa, I called Melody. I called her every day after school—just to talk. "What in the world," Mom would say to me, "can you possibly find to talk with Melody about? You just saw her at school. Is there some *new* news?"

"Mom, you just don't understand." There are some things my parents just don't understand.

"I understand why no one can ever get through to me on the phone," she'd say. "I understand that."

But today there *was* new news. Well, sort of. Melody said she heard from Renaldo, who got it straight from Jinx, who heard that Leslie told Scott (he passed it on to Jennifer) that there was going to be a special meeting of the fifth-grade music class on Monday to plan a super spectacular show to raise money for the Woodburn Community Center. Melody was out of breath from telling me about it. I was out of breath just from hearing about it! "A music show!" she squealed. "Isn't that neat?"

"I guess so," I said. I know, I should have been excited, too. But it seemed like I just hadn't had a lot of time for things like that lately. I didn't feel like hanging around school doing extra things. I don't know, I just felt like getting home. Maybe it was the divorce. Maybe it was just January.

When I walked into the kitchen, my Mom was pouring the steaming cocoa into two large mugs. She was quietly singing one of her favorite songs:

> *"I've got sunshine on a cloudy day,*
> *And when it's cold outside,*
> *I've got the month of May . . ."*

I must have heard her sing it a hundred times. It was called "My Girl," and Mom used to sing it to me as a lullaby when I was a baby. (She has such a soft, pretty voice, like marshmallows melting in steaming cocoa.) I knew the words by heart, and I found myself singing along:

> *"I guess you'll say,*
> *'What can make me feel this way?' "*

We both started to laugh. Then, Mom put her arm around my shoulder and her face next to mine, and we sang the song's refrain together:

> *"My girl, my girl, my girl,*
> *Talking 'bout my girl."*

"Ouch," Mom grimaced, "I think we need a little more practice before we're ready for the big time."

"You mean a *lot* more, don't you, Mom?" I replied.

We sat on the living room sofa watching the cold brightness of the winter day turn into the cold darkness of a winter evening. The cocoa melted the last bit of January chill inside us. It was nice, sitting there like that. Mom was softly humming again.

"You like that song a lot, don't you, Mom?" I asked.

"Hmm?" Mom said. "What song is that?"

"You know: '*My girl, my girl, my girl,*' " I sang in reply.

"Sure I do," Mom said, with a smile. "I like the songs—the songs I grew up with."

"You mean, like the golden oldies they play on the radio."

"Well," Mom said, with a quiet laugh, "they're not exactly old to me. To me, it seems just like yesterday when my girlfriends and I spent Saturday afternoons listening to our new records. Oh, and the dances. We used to practice all the latest dances: there was the twist, the mashed potato, the jerk, the Watusi"—

"The wa-whatsi?" I asked.

"The Watusi. There was— Wait a minute," she said all of a sudden. "Let me *show* you what I mean."

I tried to say "Show me what?" but Mom jumped off the sofa and headed to her bedroom in a hurry. I wondered what was on her mind as I watched the slightest sliver of a winter moon rise in the darkness outside. When Mom came back, she was holding several picture albums and a stackful of records.

"Okay, Brenda Dubrowski, on your feet!" Mom shouted.

"On my feet?"

"Let's dance down memory lane together. Come on!"

Before I could say a word, Mom grabbed me by the hand and pulled me into the middle of the living room. We pushed the furniture out of the way. "Help me roll up the rug," she said.

"Roll up the rug?" I asked. Was this my mother? The same mother who went to PTA meetings, and wore business suits to work, and hollered at the plumber.

"C'mon," she said again. "Don't be so square."

"Square?" I asked. Square? Now, what was that supposed to mean? Mom had finally flipped, I was sure. Maybe this is really an alien pretending to be my mother, I thought. But we rolled up the rug, and Mom put a record on the stereo.

"Are you ready?" Mom asked.

"Ready for what?" I asked back.

"For what?" Mom looked at me like *I* was from Mars. "Ready to rock 'n' roll! Let's dance!" I was about to say that maybe we should sit back down, sip our cocoa, and talk about this, when Mom's record took off like a shooting star. It was rock 'n' roll, all right. It was called "Rock Around the Clock." When Mom took my hand and started twirling and whirling me around the floor, I was *sure* she was an alien.

"What was that?" I asked when I finally caught my breath.

"The jitterbug," answered Mom. "That was fun, wasn't it?"

"What kind of bug?" was all I could say.

"The jitterbug. Listen to this," Mom said, putting another record on the stereo.

I couldn't believe it. "What's this one?" I asked.

"The twist." The twist? Oh, no. It sounded like a ride at the amusement park. "Here we go!" Mom shouted when the music started. And, suddenly, Mom was squirming and squiggling all over the place. Twisting, I guess. But if I hadn't seen it with my own eyes, I would never have believed it. I mean, it was like she had a bad case of fleas or something. "Like this," she said to me. "Pretend you're drying yourself with a bath towel." That's not how I dry myself, I thought. I had to admit, though, it did look like fun, and I really liked the song, too.

"Come on," Mom urged me, "let's do the twist." Oh, well, I said to myself, here goes nothing.

> *"C'mon, baby, let's do the twist,*
> *C'mon baby, let's do the twist,*
> *Take me by my little hand*
> *And go like this:*
> *Round and around and round and round we go."*

So there we were, Mom and me, twisting round and round and up and down.

We finally collapsed on the sofa. "I guess that's enough for one night," Mom said.

"No," I replied, "that's enough for one lifetime."

Mom laughed. I sat nestled next to her on the sofa for a while. My dog Muffy jumped up to snuggle in my lap. Then, Mom opened one of her photo albums. It was filled with pictures of Mom and her girlfriends when they were teenagers. I was surprised at how young my Mom looked.

"Mom," I said, surprised, "you had a ponytail."

But Mom didn't answer. One by one, she turned the pages of the albums. Sometimes, she touched a picture, as if she were trying to touch her own past. It was hard to tell if she was happy or sad. Or maybe both.

"Those days were pretty special to you, weren't they, Mom?"

"I guess they were," she said quietly. That sliver of a new moon hid itself behind a winter cloud. "You're only young once. I guess those *were* my good old days."

Mom put her arm around my shoulder. "Next to my times with you, of course," she said. I nestled closer and watched her turn the pages.

CHAPTER 3

The buzzer rang right at seven o'clock. It always did on every other Friday evening. That was my Dad coming to pick me up for the weekend. Dad was always on time. Being on time was one of the things Dad and Mom used to fight about: he always was, she usually wasn't. "Be right down, Dad," I hollered into the intercom.

"Mom, can you help me with all this stuff?" I asked. I had my overnight bag, my backpack, my flute (I just *had* to practice), and my library books for my history report.

"Are you taking enough for the weekend?" Mom asked. "Or are you and your Dad planning to go mountain climbing?" She was always kidding me about taking too much to my Dad's. But that was one of the hard things about having two homes. There are so many things you just *have* to take with you. Practical things, like my hair dryer and toothbrush. And not so practical things, like my special pillow and (don't say a word!) my very first teddy bear.

"I'll miss you a bushel and a peck," Mom said, bending down to give me a kiss goodbye. She always said goodbye to me like that. I know she missed me a lot. When I first started spending weekends with Dad, I used to call her just to say hi, and sometimes I could tell she had been crying. I could just tell. It wasn't any better when I left Dad's. He looked so sad when we had to say goodbye. The divorce was hard on all of us.

"And a hug around the neck," I always said in return.

"See you Sunday night." Mom said. "By the way," she added, handing me a big brown envelope, "would you give this to your father for me? It's just some insurance forms."

"Mom," I complained, and she knew exactly what I meant. Lisa saw how sometimes I was a—a "carrier pigeon," she called it, between my Mom and Dad. She didn't think that was a good idea—and neither did I.

"Oh, I'm sorry," Mom said at once. "I know you're right. Come on. I'll go down with you—and do it myself."

When we got out of the elevator, I raced to give my father a big hug. "How's my girl?" he said.

"Oh, she's fine," Mom answered for me. We were all quiet for a moment or two. It seemed like the icy cold weather had somehow crept inside.

"Hello, Debbie," Dad said. "How are you?"

"Oh, she's fine," I answered for her. We all started to laugh, and the ice—I mean, the ice inside—began to melt a little.

"The papers from the insurance company came yesterday, Brian," Mom said. "Would you mind looking them over?"

"Be glad to," Dad said as he took the envelope.

When Dad and I were out the door, I breathed a big sigh of relief. A *big* sigh. It's hard to explain: the colder things were between Mom and Dad, the hotter I started to feel. I felt like I couldn't breathe. I just kept waiting for them to start fighting. Sometimes it seemed like my whole life was spent either waiting for them to stop fighting or waiting for them to start. I don't know whether I wished they were still married or not.

Outside, the shock of the cold air felt really refreshing.

We hopped into Dad's car and headed for the other side of town. And before we had gone even one or two blocks, Dad said, "Hungry, honey?" and before I could even answer, Dad said, "In the mood for pizza?" and before I knew it, we were pulling up to—where else?—Polotti's Pizza Palace.

We ordered a large pizza with half mushrooms (my favorite) and half anchovies (Dad's favorite). Eating pizza with Dad was always hard. The trouble was that I hated anchovies and Dad hated mushrooms. And little bits of those disgusting fishy things were always getting on my side of the pizza and perfectly good pieces of mushroom were going to waste on Dad's side. He would pick them off and make awful faces and say, "How *do* you eat these things?" I used to say if he could eat anchovies, he should be able to eat anything. It was like a pizza civil war.

"Dad," I said, "what kind of music did you listen to when you were growing up?"

"Say what, Bren?" He was busy picking mushrooms off his half of the pizza. I asked him again. He looked up and seemed a little surprised. "Well, the same kind I listen to now, I suppose."

"Like what?"

He gave me a puzzled look. But he saw that I really wanted to know. "Well, Brenda," he began, "the music of the 1960s was really important to me"—

"Like The Beatles?" I interrupted. I knew Dad liked The Beatles. He had all their albums. He took them with him.

"Yes, like The Beatles, but there were lots of others, too."

"Why was it so important to you?"

"Not just to me," he explained. "It was important to a whole generation of young people, a generation looking for . . . looking for . . . something."

I asked: "Looking for what?"

Dad thought for a while. "I'm not sure I know," he finally said. "I sure thought I knew then, though." Dad took a bite of pizza, keeping an eye out for mushrooms. "What were we looking for? That's a hard one. You might say we were looking for a kind of freedom, the freedom to be what we wanted to be. Not just what our parents and teachers wanted us to be. And rock 'n' roll was a second national anthem for us, our Star Spangled Banner. A way to say we were different, we were independent. I even played the guitar a little myself. Does that make any sense?"

"Not really," I said.

Dad smiled and then leaned over to whisper. "Want to know something else?"

I leaned over, too. "What?"

"Back in those days, your Dad had a ponytail."

"A ponytail!" I shouted in surprise, loud enough for everyone in Polotti's to hear. "You mean, you were a hippie?"

"Well, uh, yeah, I guess I was."

"I don't believe it," I said, laughing. "Wait till all my friends find out."

Dad smiled again before asking, "What's this all about?"

I wasn't sure what it was all about. "Were those your good old days?" I asked.

"My good old days?" asked Dad, looking more puzzled than before. "I don't know about that," he replied. "It was a time I'll never forget, that's for sure. Back then, I don't know, the world seemed so new and exciting. I guess you *could* say those were my good old days. I guess so. But, Brenda, honey, any day with you is a good old day to me. Now, if you don't want your friends to laugh, you'd better keep this hippie business to yourself. And you'd better start eating that pizza. The only thing worse than a mushroom pizza is a *cold* mushroom pizza."

CHAPTER 4

Ms. Farrow brought the Monday meeting of the fifth-grade music class to order. Of course, the news of the show had spread all over Woodburn. The Woodburn School was funny that way. Mark Riley used to say that we didn't need a school newspaper: "All we have to do is tell Melody something, and it'll be front-page news in no time."

Ms. Farrow explained that the music show would help raise funds to remodel the Woodburn day care center and to buy new playground stuff for the little kids. She even showed us a picture of the biggest, neatest jungle gym you ever saw. "That's great," Scott said, and everyone agreed. The way we oohed and ahhed, you'd think the jungle gym was for us. I think we almost wished it was.

"So we better have a really great show," Ms. Farrow said. "Now, we have a lot of work to do. But the very first thing we need, I think, is to find a theme for the show."

"What kind of theme?" Renaldo asked.

"Use your imagination," encouraged Ms. Farrow.

"What about The Wild West?" Nam asked. "We could build a wagon train and sing cowboy songs."

"Cowboy songs?" I asked. "What kinds of songs would a cowboy sing?"

Robbie spoke too soon for Nam to answer. "I have an even better idea," Robbie offered. "What about a combat theme? We could dress up in army fatigues, and"—

"Uh, I don't think so, Robbie," Ms. Farrow said. No matter what we were doing, Robbie thought it was a good idea to wear army uniforms.

"I like a beach idea," Leslie said. "What if we put on a June in January show? We could wear bathing suits"—

"Hey, it's cold out there," Renaldo protested. "I'm keeping my clothes on, if you don't mind."

There were other ideas, too. I was listening, but I was also thinking. Thinking about my Mom doing the twist. Thinking about my Dad the hippie. Thinking about how things must have been when . . . well, I was thinking about a lot of things. And, somehow, someway, my hand was in the air.

"Brenda?" Ms. Farrow asked.

"Yes, Ms. Farrow?"

"Your hand? Do you have an idea for the show's theme?"

"Oh, . . . well, what about a show of golden oldies? You know, like the songs our parents used to listen to."

"Yeah," Scott said, "there's a radio station like that: *'More rock, less talk: the hits from the '50s and the '60s on the only all*

Oldie/Goldie station.' " It was funny. He sounded just like the guy on the radio. "My older brother listens to that all the time."

"I think that's a good idea," said Jennifer.

"We could call it 'The Good Old Days,' " I suggested.

"And we could keep our clothes on," Renaldo added.

"Why, that is a *very* good idea, Brenda," Ms. Farrow said. "Hmm . . . 'The Good Old Days': very creative, indeed!"

"But, Ms. Farrow," Melody asked, "how are we going to sing all the songs? How are we going to play all the music?"

"That's easy," Scott said. "We'll do what my brother does. He sings along with the radio and pretends to be playing the guitar. He calls it 'lip-synching.' I call it weird."

"We'll make a tape of our favorite golden oldies," I said. "My parents have lots of records we could borrow."

"My father has a set of drums in the basement," said Brian. "We could use them and pretend to play along with the tape."

"That's a great idea!" exclaimed Ms. Farrow. "What about your brother's guitar, Scott?"

"Guitar?" Scott replied. "He doesn't have a guitar. He plays a broom. I told you: weird."

"I think my father might still have his guitar," I said.

"I'll lend my clarinet," said Jinx.

"And my saxophone," added Brian.

"You can use my tape recorder," Melody said.

"Good. Then, it's settled," said a delighted Ms. Farrow to everyone's satisfaction. " 'The Good Old Days' are back!"

"Did you have any good old days, Ms. Farrow?" Leslie asked.

"Of course, I did, Leslie," she replied. "I wasn't born a music teacher, you know. That's why this is such a wonderful idea for our music show. We all have our good old days."

"*I* don't remember any good old days," said Robbie glumly.

"Well, I do," Renaldo said.

"You do?" wondered Ms. Farrow.

"Sure," Renaldo replied. "Ah, the carefree days of first grade. Those were the good old days."

"Well, before we get lost in the long ago," Ms. Farrow said, trying to hide a smile, "let's remember that the show is going to be a lot of hard work. And everyone is going to have to pitch in. I have a long list of jobs here." She was right: there *was* a lot to do. "Someone has to be in charge of publicity."

"I'll take that one," said Mark Riley. "My Cruiser and I will get the word out in a hurry." Mark's Cruiser was his wheelchair. "The fastest pair of wheels in Woodburn," Mark always said.

"But not *too* big a hurry, Mark," Ms. Farrow cautioned him. "Now, someone has to sell tickets."

"Here I am," Renaldo spoke up. "Ready to sell, sell, sell. And sell. Don't worry about a thing. This show will be SRO—that's Standing Room Only—in no time."

"Renaldo thinks he's a business genius," Jinx laughed.

"And you know what they say," Renaldo replied, " 'there's no business like show business.' "

"And now for the really big job," Ms. Farrow said. "Who's going to direct the show? Someone has to select the acts and lead the rehearsals. Who's going to be in charge of the show?"

Suddenly, it got very quiet. No one raised a hand.

Robbie broke the silence. "Whose idea was this anyway?"

Just as suddenly, everyone was looking at me.

"Well, Brenda?" was all Ms. Farrow said.

But that was all she had to say. Director of the music show! I was so excited I just couldn't say no. I didn't want to say no. Think of it, I said to myself, my own show. Director of the Woodburn musical! Of course, I said, "Yes." Yes, yes, yes.

This would be *my* show. I couldn't wait to tell my Mom and Dad. They would be so proud. I wanted them to sit in the front row. I wondered: when was the last time they did something special together? I couldn't even remember. But this is different, I thought. This would be like . . . well, like the good old days before they were divorced. Just for one night.

That's all I asked for: the good old days for one special night.

CHAPTER 5

The buzzer went off right at seven o'clock.

"Dad," I whispered into the intercom, "could you come up for a while?" I knew he wouldn't like that.

I could tell Mom didn't like the idea much either. "I need to speak with both of you," I explained. I remembered what Lisa said about talking things out. "Okay, let's talk," I said to myself.

We sat at the kitchen table. "Well, what's this all about?" Dad asked. He was jingling the change in his pocket. He did that when he was nervous.

Mom raised her hands in a way that meant, "It's a mystery to me." She was drumming her fingers on the table. She did that when she was nervous.

"I know you don't do a lot together anymore," I began, "but I want you both to come to the fifth-grade music show at Woodburn. Because I'm the director and"—

I didn't get a chance to finish because Mom and Dad were both shouting "Congratulations!" and "Hey, that's great!" I knew they would be happy for me.

"Then, you'll come?" I asked.

"You can bet on it," Dad said.

"Wild horses couldn't keep me away," Mom assured me.

"Phew," I said, "I'm glad that's settled." Okay, let's keep talking. "I want you to sit in the front row." Mom and Dad grew kind of quiet. Then, I said the big "T" word: "Together."

"Together?" Mom asked.

"Together?" Dad asked.

"Together," I said.

"Oh, Brenda," Mom said, "I don't know. I mean, you know"—

Dad felt the same way. "You know that's just not the way it is," he tried to explain.

"My friend Amelia might like to come along with me," Mom added.

I was getting angry. "You can bring your friends to something else," I insisted. "But this is different: this is special." I felt like a parent with her two little children. "Dad, I want you to go with Mom," I said. "And, Mom, I want you to go with Dad. That's all there is to it."

"Just a minute, Brenda," Dad said, "your mother and I will both be there"—

Mom finished the sentence for him: "We just won't be there together."

I wasn't *getting* angry now: I *was* angry, and I wanted them to know I was angry. I walked out of the room, and I made sure to slam the door behind me. So much for one special night.

CHAPTER 6

In just a few days, the music show was a big hit at Woodburn. A big hit? It was a home run with the bases loaded! You wouldn't have recognized the place. Wherever you turned, people were singing, whistling, or humming their favorite songs. Everyone was getting into the act. Every last person!

Friday was tryout day for the show. I set up a desk near Mr. Beame's classroom and asked Jennifer to be my assistant. By the time we got there, there was already a line of people waiting to sign up. I blew my whistle (I borrowed it from Coach Kontos) and asked for quiet.

Brian, Jason, Scott, and Robbie were first in line. They were going to be The Beatles. The only thing was, they couldn't decide which Beatle they were going to be.

"I'm John," Robbie said proudly.

"I thought *I* was John," said Brian.

"No, you're Ringo," Jason replied.

"I'm supposed to be Ringo!" hollered Scott.

"Who's George?" asked Brian.

"You're George," answered Robbie.

"He's Paul," Scott insisted.

It was too confusing. "Will you just have it straightened out by rehearsal time, guys?" I asked. "Next."

Renaldo was next. "Brenda," he halfway whispered, "I want to be in the show, but I'm not so sure"—

"Renaldo," I said, quickly interrupting him, "I have just the thing for you. You can be Stevie Wonder. It's perfect."

But Renaldo wasn't crazy about the idea. "Just because I'm blind doesn't mean I have to be Stevie Wonder, does it? Now, Michael Jackson," he said, "that's another story. I'm so baaaaad!"

"Believe him, Brenda," Jennifer said, laughing. "He is bad. I've heard him sing."

"Could we try to be serious for just a minute?" I asked. "All right, Renaldo," I continued, "the show needs someone to introduce the acts."

"You mean a master of ceremonies? The MC?"

"That's right," I said. "Can you do the job?"

"Can I do it? Listen to this: 'Ladies and gentlemen' "—

"Fine," I said, interrupting him again. "I'll put you down for MC. Thank you. Next."

Mark and Michael Riley wanted to sing the theme song from the "Mister Ed" television show. You know, the one about the talking horse. I mean, how silly can you get! "That's not a *real* song," I argued.

"Of course, it is," Michael said. "Isn't it, Mark?"

"Of course," Mark echoed.

"Did you say, 'Of course'?" Michael asked, and before I could say another word, they began to sing:

> *"A horse is a horse, of course, of course,*
> *And no one can talk to a horse, of course,*
> *Unless, of course, the name of the horse*
> *Is the famous Mister Ed."*

"I know the song," I said impatiently. "But it doesn't really count"—

"Yeah, quit horsing around," Renaldo joked.

"It's okay, Brenda," Jennifer started to say, but I stopped her with my best "don't butt in" glare.

"Well, what about 'The Flintstones' song?" Mark asked.

They were about to sing again when I stopped them. "That's enough," I said. It's no wonder Mom doesn't like me to watch too much television, I thought. "Put the Rileys down for 'Mister Ed.'"

"Oh, Brenda," Michael said, "just one more thing."

"What's that?" I asked.

"Yabba, dabba, do!"

"Next!"

Next was Melody.

"Yes, Melody?" I asked. I hadn't been director for very long, but my patience was already wearing thin.

"I want to be The Supreme," Melody said proudly.

"You want to be the what?"

"You know, The Supreme," she repeated.

"No, I don't know," I insisted.

"Oh, Brenda," Melody said to me. "You know their songs." She leaned over and in a whisper sang the words to "Where Did Our Love Go?" "You know," she said again.

"That's The Supremes, Melody. There were three of them."

"I know that. But there's only one of me."

"Well, that's too bad, Melody. It's either three Supremes or no Supremes. Next."

Melody looked like she might cry, when Jennifer butted in again. "I'll be in it with you, Mel," Jennifer said. Her voice was all excitement. "My Mom used to love The Supremes."

"That's still only two," I said. "You need one more Supreme."

"We'll find one more, won't we, Jennifer?" Melody said with a note of hope in her voice.

But before Jennifer could answer, I hollered, "Next!"

There was still a long line of people waiting to sign up. Even Mrs. Rothman from the Senior Center wanted to be a part of the show. "I could do the Charleston. It was *the* dance in my day."

"I'm sorry," I said to Mrs. Rothman. I thought I had heard everything. "But it's just not the same"—

"But, Brenda," Jennifer said before I could put my glare to work, "those were *her* good old days."

"All right," I said impatiently, "put Mrs. Rothman down for the Charleston." I was beginning to regret that I had ever made Jennifer my assistant. After all, I was the director, wasn't I? An assistant was supposed to assist, right? "Next," I grumbled.

"Pssst."

Leslie stepped up to the desk.

"Pssst."

"What is that 'psssting' sound?" I asked Jennifer.

"Pssst." There it was again. "Brenda. Over here." It was Mr. Beame. His head was just barely sticking out of his classroom door, and he was waving for me to come in. Now what? Oh, goodness, I thought, the things a director has to do. "Just a second, Leslie," I said. "I'll be right back."

"Shut the door," Mr. Beame whispered as soon as I was in his office. I was beginning to worry. Maybe the show had to be cancelled. But it wasn't that. It wasn't that at all.

"Have a seat, Brenda," Mr. Beame said politely.

"Is something wrong?" I asked.

"Well, no."

"But you wanted to see me."

"Well, yes. You see . . . that is . . . I was wondering: do you think *I* could sign up for a part in the show?"

"*You* want to be in the show?"

"Do you think it would be all right?"

"I don't know. It's really for the"—

"I thought I would be Elvis Presley."

I almost fell off my chair. Now, I guess I *had* heard everything. "You want to be Elvis Presley?"

"I know it's a little unusual," he said quietly.

A little? What's next? I asked myself. Maybe Dr. Mathewson, the school principal, would want to wear a miniskirt and do the hula-hoop. What was happening to this school, anyway?

"I'm sorry, Mr. Beame," I said, "but the show is really for the fifth grade." I wasn't going to tell him about the Charleston.

"Of course," he said. "I understand. It's your show, after all."

Mr. Beame looked awfully disappointed, and I felt a little sorry for him. But Mr. Beame as Elvis? That was too much. And it *was* my show, after all.

By the time I got back to the sign-up desk, things were out of hand. Completely out of hand. What a racket! The Beatles still couldn't figure out who was who. Michael and Mark were singing that stupid "Mister Ed" song. Melody and Jennifer were looking for a third Supreme. And Mrs. Rothman was busy practicing the Charleston.

I could see right then and there that I was going to have to take charge of this show. I was going to have to take charge once and for all.

"Listen up," I shouted above the noise. "Rehearsal is next Monday night, and I want to see these acts ready. Is that clear?" I blew my whistle, just to make sure they got the point.

Renaldo snapped to attention and pretended to salute. "Yes, sir," he said. "I mean, yes, Miss Director . . . I mean . . . oh, Brenda, you know what I mean." I heard my friends giggling and snickering.

"Was that supposed to be some kind of a joke, Renaldo?" I asked angrily.

"It wasn't supposed to be some kind of anything," Renaldo said back. "What's the matter with you?"

I didn't answer him. What was the matter with *me*? There was nothing the matter with me. So what *was* the matter? The matter was that I was trying to put on my show, that's all. I was just trying to put on my show. My fists were clenched in tight little knots.

I felt someone tugging on me.

"What do you want, Nam?" I snapped.

"I, uh, just wanted," he stammered, "to be a cowboy."

"And I suppose you'll want to bring a live cow on the stage," I said.

"Hey," Renaldo said to me, "what's your beef?"

I started to say "That's not funny," but everybody started to crowd around and shout out ideas. Their own silly ideas.

"I want to do a surfer song," Leslie said. "Can I bring in my little sister's sandbox and a beach umbrella and"—

"That's the dumbest thing I ever heard," I said. "I won't have that in my show."

"Can I do a ballet act?" Christine asked.

"Can I dress up like G.I. Joe?" (Guess who that was?)

"Can I sing like The Chipmunks?"

"Can I be President Kennedy?"

"Can I . . . can I . . . can I?"

"That's enough!" I said at the top of my voice. The show was getting out of control, and I was nearly crying. "You're ruining it, all of you. You don't understand." Now, *I* was getting out of control, and I think I *was* crying. "I want my parents to be here. In the front row. Together. And now you're ruining everything!"

I threw my whistle on the ground and stormed out.

CHAPTER 7

"I told you it was a long story," I said to Lisa. "Did I forget to mention that it didn't have a happy ending?"

"Well," Lisa replied, "lots of things in real life don't. That's part of what makes real life more interesting than a story."

"If you say so," I answered. "But why did they have to ruin it for me? It isn't fair. They knew how much it meant to me."

"How did they know?" asked Lisa. "Did you tell them?"

"No, I didn't really tell them," I answered. "But they knew my parents would be there."

"And so?" Lisa asked to my surprise.

"And so, so what?"

"What I mean," Lisa replied, "is that all your friends would have *their* parents there, wouldn't they?"

"Yes, but that's different."

"Why? I'm sure your friends would want to impress their parents, too."

"It's different because . . . because my parents are divorced."

The room grew silent. I knew that Lisa would let the silence do its slow, quiet work.

"Brenda," she finally said, "do you remember how you felt when your parents first separated?"

"Yes," I said. "It was terrible."

"What was the worst part?"

"The worst part? Well, I don't know. There were lots of bad parts. I remember all the fighting. That was bad. I thought I would get sick to my stomach when I heard them fighting like that. Some nights, I would lie awake listening to them, and I was scared. I was scared what would happen. I was scared they wouldn't stop.

"I remember lots of whispering back and forth. I didn't know what was going on and I didn't know what was going to happen. That was a worst part, too. I remember when Mom and Dad told me about the divorce—that they wouldn't be living together. I just couldn't understand what they were saying. I mean, I knew what they were saying, but it just didn't make any sense. My parents living apart: what would happen to me? It didn't make any sense at all.

"I don't know what the worst part was. But I know I felt so torn, like I was being split apart. If I was for my Mom, it felt like I was against Dad. If I was for my Dad, it felt like I was against Mom. It was like a tug-of-war with me in the middle. Sometimes, I felt like I was being torn in two."

Sitting there with Lisa, I remembered the fear and sadness. But I didn't just remember those feelings. I could still *feel* them. I could still feel how confused I was. *What was going to happen to me?* I could still feel how embarrassed I was. *What would I tell my friends?* Sitting there with Lisa, I felt myself fill up again with that same fear, that same sadness. I was angry—angry with myself. I wanted to have these feelings under control. Brenda Dubrowski, I said to myself, what's the matter with you? But it was no use. It was like I had a tight grip on my feelings, but I couldn't hold on. I just couldn't.

"Maybe the worst part," I said, "was that everything seemed so out of control. Like the feeling you get on a wild ride at the amusement park. Only this was for real. And it wouldn't stop."

"That's a scary feeling, isn't it?" Lisa asked. It was a question I didn't have to answer. "Is it better now?"

"I guess it's better," I said, but I only halfway meant it. "But I'm still in the middle. Like the show. Who else has to worry how their parents are going to . . . to behave? Why do *I* have to? Why do I always have to be in charge of them?" I saw that my fists were tight little knots again. "I guess that's why I wanted everything about the show to be just right. That's why I wanted things to be perfect . . . for one night."

"Well, Brenda," Lisa said, "that's not the way things are. You can't make them perfect. You'll only make yourself miserable."

"Not to mention all of my friends."

"Not to mention your friends," agreed Lisa. "Brenda, when you were so confused about the divorce, what did you do?"

"I did what you said. You told me to talk to my parents, to tell them how I felt."

"Did that help?"

"Yes," I said. "It helped a lot."

"Do you think it might help to talk with them again?"

"I guess so."

"Do you think it might help to talk to your friends?"

"I guess it couldn't hurt."

"Do you know what you'll say to them?"

"I guess I could start with 'I'm sorry.' "

Lisa smiled. "That *would* be a good place to start," she said.

CHAPTER 8

It *was* a good place to start. The only thing was, I wasn't the one who started.

I was a few minutes late for our next rehearsal. I was too busy rehearsing my apology. I still didn't know exactly what I was going to say when I walked backstage. I saw everybody talking together. It was a kind of meeting or something. I figured they probably wanted a new director.

It was Robbie who started. "Brenda, we've been talking," he said, "and we want to apologize."

"*You* want to apologize?" I asked in disbelief.

"Yes," he said. "I guess we've been . . . um . . . Jennifer, what did you call it?"

Jennifer said: "Insensitive."

"Oh, yeah," Robbie went on. "I guess we've been insensitive. We just didn't realize how much this show means to you. With your Mom and Dad split up . . . and, well"—

"What Robbie is trying to say," Jennifer explained, "is that we'll do the show the way you want it." Jennifer handed me my whistle and megaphone. "We're sorry we made such a mess of things," she added.

"No more jokes," said Renaldo.

"No more horsing around," said Mark.

"Wait a minute," I said. "I think you've got things a little backwards. I'm the one who should apologize. I tried to make the show *my* show. I don't even know why. I guess I wanted . . . well,

I guess I know what I wanted. But it was wrong—it wasn't fair. I'm the one who's sorry. I took all the fun out of it."

"That's for sure," mumbled Renaldo.

"No, you didn't," said Melody, glaring at Renaldo.

"Yes, I did," I said. "It's not *my* show. It's *our* show. And if Mark and Michael want to be 'Mister Ed,' that's okay with me."

"You mean it?" they asked together.

"Of course, I mean it," I was happy to say.

I turned to Melody and Jennifer. "And two Supremes are better than none," I said.

"You mean it?" they asked together.

"I mean it!"

I saw Mrs. Rothman with a "What about me?" look on her face. "And, Mrs. Rothman," I said, "would you do the Charleston?"

"You mean it?" she asked.

"Definitely. Absolutely. Positively. I mean it!"

"I think she means it," Renaldo said.

"Hooray for Brenda," everyone shouted. "On with the show!"

It was funny. I was giving up control of the show, and yet I felt more in control than ever. I felt that, somehow, it would all work out. And if it didn't, well, at least I would still have my friends. At least I would have fun.

"Thanks," I said. "But we have a lot work to do, don't we? So let's get going."

"Yes, Your Directorship," said Renaldo, saluting me. I heard my friends laughing at Renaldo's antics. But this time it was different. This time, I heard myself laughing, too.

CHAPTER 9

Just one special night. That's what I wrote in my letter. I guess it seems odd to write a letter to my Mom and Dad. It *is* kind of odd, but sometimes it's hard to get them together. And I thought that if I said what I had to say in a letter, maybe they would really listen to it.

Dear Mom and Dad,

Wouldn't it be nice if just for one special night we could bring back the good old days? If just for one special night, we could be together again.

I know we can't really bring back the past. I know that we can't bring back our old family again and have our old family times. I know I have to stop wishing for that.

But we are still a family—and we can have new family times, if we really want to. Sometimes together, and sometimes not. I know, now, that the together part is up to you.

Together or not, you are special guests for a special show:

Invitation

What?: "The Good Old Days: A Musical Revue"

Where?: The Woodburn School Auditorium

When?: January 21, 7:00 pm

Who?: Ms. Farrow's fifth-grade music class

And the best part of all is that "The Good Old Days" is directed by your one and only daughter, Brenda Dubrowski! It's directed with love from me to you.

Brenda

CHAPTER 10

The next few weeks went by in a blur of activity. There really was a lot of work to do: rehearsing the acts, taping the songs, designing the stage, writing the program. Woodburn was a whirlwind of singing and dancing, guitars and drums, rock groups and TV shows. It was a whirlwind of fun.

I hadn't said a word to either Mom or Dad about the tickets, and they hadn't said a word to me.

Finally, it was the night of the big show. I drove with Ms. Farrow to get there early. We still had a lot of work to do to get things ready. I kept peeking behind the stage curtain to watch the audience grow and grow. My jitters were growing, too.

Renaldo was right about the SRO part. It *was* standing room only. I peeked behind the curtain one more time and . . . there they were! Mom and Dad were sitting in the front row together. "This is it," I whispered to myself. I took a deep breath, crossed my fingers on both hands, and went backstage.

"Okay, Renaldo," I urged, "let's go."

"Go where?" he asked.

"It's show time!" I exclaimed. All of a sudden, Renaldo—Mr. Show Business—looked nervous.

"Don't forget your lines," Robbie teased him.

"Don't sweat it," answered Renaldo. "I have them written in Braille on little cards."

"Break a leg, kiddo," said Mrs. Rothman. All of a sudden, Renaldo looked *very* nervous.

"Don't worry, Renaldo," I assured him. "She just means good luck." I patted him on the back and whispered in his ear: "You can do it. I know you can."

Renaldo walked to center stage and reached into his pocket for his Braille cards. The crowd grew quiet when he started to speak. "Ladies and gentlemen," Renaldo began, "the Woodburn School fifth-grade music class is proud to bring you our winter musical, an extravaganza of song and dance from 'The Good Old Days.' And, now, for our first act, please welcome that fabulous foursome: Brian, Scott, Jason, and Robbie . . . otherwise known as The Beatles."

There was loud applause from the audience. And there were cheers for different Beatles. There were whistles from the crowd. But there were no Beatles.

Renaldo cleared his throat. Then, he said again: "Otherwise known as The Beatles."

There was more applause, more cheers, more whistles. But there were still no Beatles.

I heard Renaldo say "Pardon me" to the crowd and tiptoe backstage. "What is going on?" a desperate Renaldo asked. "I'm dying out there."

"It's the tape," Jennifer explained. "Something's wrong with the tape."

"That can't be," Renaldo said, "we checked it out last night."

"Well, check it out now," she said back, holding up strands and strands of tape. "The tape player ate it," she explained.

"Looks more like it chewed it up and spit it out," added a disappointed Robbie.

"Oh," Renaldo groaned, "I'm almost glad I can't see it."

"What a mess!" said Jason. "There goes the show."

"There goes the show," echoed Melody.

I saw "There goes the show" written on the faces of all my friends.

"Wait," I suddenly said. "We can't give up now."

"But, Brenda," Jennifer said, "there's no tape."

"No tape, no show," Robbie moaned.

"There has to be a way," I insisted. "If we just pull together, we'll find a way." I turned to Renaldo. "Renaldo," I pleaded, "go back on stage and stall for time."

"Stall for time?" Renaldo asked. "How?"

I put my arm on Renaldo's shoulder and gave him the best advice I could: "Think of something."

Renaldo tiptoed back to center stage and, one more time, cleared his throat. "Hmm, hmmm. Ladies and gentlemen, there's been a slight problem. Technical difficulties: that kind of thing. But nothing to worry about. It reminds me of the story . . ."

Oh, no, I thought. He was going to tell them his jokes! I had to act fast. I stuck my head around the stage and tried to get Mr. Beame's attention.

"Pssst, Mr. Beame," I whispered. "Over here."

"Brenda," he said to me in a low voice, "what's going on?"

"*You're* going on, Mr. Beame," I said. "You're going on now." Then, I added: "Please?"

"What?" he exclaimed.

"You wanted to be Elvis. Now's your chance. Please."

"Well, uh, Brenda, now, I really don't know."

"Mr. Beame, we really need you. We need you to be Elvis!" I almost had to drag him backstage, but get him backstage I did.

"Well, uh, if you really insist," he said as I was "insisting" him onto the stage. "After all, the show must go on."

I was almost out of breath as I whispered to Renaldo from behind the stage curtain. "Renaldo, Mr. Beame is going to be Elvis Presley."

"Ha, ha," Renaldo laughed. "Brenda, that's a good one. Mr. Beame as Elvis Presley. Ha, ha. I wish I had thought of that."

"Renaldo Rodriguez," I said sternly, "I'm not kidding. Mr. Beame is going on as Elvis."

Renaldo faced the crowd with a slight smile. "Ladies and gentlemen: there has been a minor change of plans. We have a very special star with us tonight. May I present none other than The King of Rock 'n' Roll himself, Mr. Elvis Presley."

Mr. Beame walked onstage looking nervous, to say the least. His knees were knocking so hard I thought he might hurt himself. But he took a deep breath, gulped two or three times, and started to sing, "You Ain't Nothin' But A Hound Dog."

The crowd started to clap in time, and that seemed to give Mr. Beame the encouragement he needed. Then, he started to shake his hips. No kidding: Mr. Beame was shaking his hips! "Lord, have mercy!" someone shouted out from the crowd. Other people started to shout, "Elvis! Elvis!" Suddenly, Brian's father was standing behind me. "Anyone need a drummer?" he asked. I didn't have time to answer that one: I just pushed him in the right direction. "Brian, Jennifer, go on out and play your instruments. Maybe we've lost our tape, but we've gained a band!"

There may not have been a lot of show to steal, but what there was Mr. Beame stole with a flourish. By the time he was done, I think he broke every heart in the audience. He sang "Jailhouse Rock" and "Love Me Tender," and it was all Renaldo could do to get him off the stage finally. And *that* was just the beginning. The Beatles sang, and Michael and Mark did their "Mister Ed" thing. Melody and Jennifer pretended they were the two Supremes, and Leslie sang under her beach umbrella. And Mrs. Rothman kicked up her heels and taught us all how to do the Charleston.

And *that* wasn't all. What happened next is hard to describe. It's still hard for me to believe. But, one by one, teachers and parents and sisters and brothers took turns singing and dancing

"The Good Old Days"

and playing in the band. Brian's father performed a drum solo, and Leslie's mother showed us how to do the locomotion (it was so much fun), Dr. Mathewson and Ms. Ricci sang folk songs, and my Mom and Dad, my very own Mom and Dad, danced the best jitterbug you ever saw. It was unbelievable! "On with the show!" I said to myself.

I stood off in the wing of the stage and watched it all happen. There seemed to be more people on the stage than in the audience. I watched them all having a good time. And I watched my Mom and Dad having a good time, too—with each other. You know, I enjoyed that: just watching it all happen.

CHAPTER 11

I had to stay after the show to help clean up. Mom and Dad pitched in to make the work go faster.

I don't really know why they had to get divorced. But I guess it had to happen. I wish they could have been happy together. I used to wish all the time that we would be a family again—the three of us.

"See you Friday night, honey," Dad said, after the job was done. He turned to Mom and said simply, "Thanks, Debbie."

And she replied, "Thank you."

I know that we really are a family. Not the kind we were, not the regular kind (oh, you know what I mean), but the kind where—well, where there's love, and where there's sharing, and where you care about each other.

"Cocoa tonight?" Mom asked on our way out.

"With or without?" I asked back.

"With, of course," she said.

"You bet," I answered.

Lisa says life isn't perfect. Things change, and we don't always know why. Things change, and we can't always control the way they change. Sometimes, we have to change, too, and that can be scary.

I took one last look at the empty stage on our way out. I closed my eyes, and (just for a moment) I could see "The Good Old Days" happen all over again. A moment later, and the stage was empty.

"Brenda," Mom called to me, "time to get a move on."

She was right, of course. It was time to get on with the show.

Questions for Brenda

Many kids have questions about divorce. You may have a question, too.

Q. Why did your Mom and Dad get a divorce?

A. I don't really know for sure because some of the reasons are really personal to them. Mom told me they couldn't agree on the kinds of things that are so important to a happy marriage: things like how to spend money, or what things to do together, or how to bring up children. Dad said pretty much the same thing. He said they were just too different to stay married.

Q. Did you ever feel the divorce was your fault?

A. Sometimes I did. I thought: maybe if I could just be a better kid, they would stay together. But now I know that isn't true. Lisa, my counselor, says it's normal for kids to feel that way. They get caught in the middle of a grown-up problem and blame themselves.

Sometimes, when Mom and Dad were arguing a lot, I would write them little "Please don't fight" or "Please be nice" notes. Now, I see that I was trying to keep them from getting divorced. But I was just putting myself in the middle again by doing that.

Kids don't make their parents get divorced, and they can't make them stay together. As Lisa says: "It's not your decision, and it's not your fault."

Q. How did you find out your parents were getting a divorce?

A. I was nine years old when my parents told me they were going to separate. They said they were going to live apart for a while to see if they really wanted to get a divorce. I knew they weren't very happy, but when I asked them about it, they would always say, "Grown-up problems, honey." Or something like that.

But when they decided to separate, they told me together— without fighting for a change. I felt a lot of things when they told me. I was confused and hurt and mad and embarrassed. But I was glad to know the truth. And it was good that we could talk about it together.

Q. Who takes care of you?

A. When parents get divorced, they have to decide which one of them will have "custody" of their child or children. Custody means who is going to be responsible for the child. My Mom and Dad decided on what is called "joint custody." That's where both parents help raise the child. There are other kinds of custody. One of these is called "sole custody" or "single-parent custody." That's where only one parent is in charge.

I'm glad both Mom and Dad are in charge of me. There are a lot of big decisions to make, like what summer camp I go to or how much allowance I get. It's easier for me because my Mom and Dad make these decisions together. That's what works best for us. But it's up to each family to decide what works best for them.

Q. But who do you live with?

A. Mom and Dad talked a lot about that. They finally decided it would be best for me to live mostly with my Mom. But I see my Dad every Wednesday night and live with him every other weekend. I spend half the summer with him, too, and the other half with Mom. It wasn't easy for me at first, going back and forth from Mom to Dad and Dad to Mom. Sometimes, I felt like a ping-pong ball.

I can still remember the first few months after the divorce. There were lots of problems. Like, Dad would feel that he and I had to do about a million things on the weekends I spent with him. One weekend we went to the zoo, on a picnic, to the movies, out to dinner—and that was only Saturday! He was trying to make up for the time we *don't* get to spend together, I guess. But it sure was exhausting!

Or when Mom and Dad talked to one another *through me*. Do you know what I mean? It's "Would you tell your Mom this?" or "Let your Dad know this." Or Mom would ask me questions about Dad, and Dad would ask me about Mom: that's what Lisa means by me being a "carrier pigeon." Talk about being in the middle! I felt like a ping-pong ball with ears.

But it's working out pretty well now. With Lisa's help, I was able to tell Mom and Dad how I felt about these things. I could tell my Dad that, lots of times, I liked just being with him—without millions of things to do. And I could tell both of them to talk to each other, without putting me in the middle.

And, with Lisa's help, Mom and Dad were able to listen. Talking and listening: it's made all the difference in the world.

Q. Did you get to pick who to live with?

A. No, and I'm glad I didn't. What would I have done if they had asked me? It would seem like I was picking the parent I liked the best or loved the most. But that's not the way it is with me. I don't want to pick sides: I like them both the same. And I love them both the same, too. The last thing in the world I would want is to choose between them. If they had asked me to decide, I would have said, "No." I would have told them to make that decision together.

Q. But who pays for all the things you need?

A. Dad and Mom both pay. It works this way. Because I live most of the time with Mom, she has most of the expenses to support me. There are lots of expenses, like clothes and food and rent. So Dad makes a special payment each month to Mom just to help with my expenses. That's called "child support."

When parents divorce, they often fight about child support. Even though my parents agreed on the child support payments, I still hear Mom mumbling sometimes about not getting enough from Dad, or Dad grumbling now and again about paying too much to Mom. I hear it, but I try not to listen to it. I figure that money is something for them to talk about to each other, not to me. The only thing I really want to hear about money is a raise in my allowance. How about it, Mom and Dad?

Q. Did you have to go to court?

A. No, because my parents were able to agree on custody and child support. But it's not always that easy. What if they didn't agree? Then, they would go to court, where a judge would listen to them and decide what was best. Sometimes, a judge will want to talk with the child or children, too, before deciding who should have custody. I think that would be the hardest part of a divorce on a kid.

Q. Why do you go to a counselor?

A. I go to see Lisa Bell, my counselor, because she gives me good ideas on how to solve problems. She shows me how to talk with my parents in ways that really work. And counseling gives me a chance just to talk about how I feel. Whenever I have a problem, with my parents or with other things, I can go to Lisa. It helps me a lot.

And even though I'm older now, I still talk with Lisa about the divorce. Lisa explained to me that there is no magic time when you can say, "I'm over the divorce now. It's all in the past." As you get older, there will be new feelings to talk about. So it's nice to know Lisa will be there.

Q. Do you ever wish your parents would get back together?

A. At first, I wished that all the time. When I blew out my birthday candles, that's what I wished for. When I found a four-leaf clover or saw a shooting star, that's what I wished for. But, of course, it didn't happen, and after a while I knew it wasn't going to happen.

But I don't wish for that anymore. Maybe I wanted them to get back together so much because I was thinking so much about me. I wanted things to be just the way they were. But, you know, the way things were wasn't so good. Not for Mom or Dad. Not for me, either. And, now, both Mom and Dad seem happier. Come to think of it, I'm happier, too.

Sometimes, I still wish I had a "regular" family, but, now, I know that the best kind of family is one where people love each other and care for each other. The best kind of family is one where people show each other the love and caring they feel, one where deep down in their hearts (where it really matters) they want the best for each other. That's the kind of family I want. And that's the kind of family I have!

About The Kids on the Block

Founded in 1977 by Barbara Aiello, The Kids on the Block puppet program was formed to introduce young audiences to the topic of children with disabilities. Since then the goals and programs of The Kids on the Block have evolved and broadened to encompass a wide spectrum of individual differences and social concerns.

Barbara Aiello is nationally recognized for her work in special education. The former editor of *Teaching Exceptional Children*, Ms. Aiello has won numerous awards for her work with The Kids on the Block, including the President's Committee on Employment of the Handicapped Distinguished Service Award, the Easter Seal Communications Award for Outstanding Public Service, and the Epilepsy Foundation of America's Outstanding Achievement Award. Her puppets have appeared in all 50 states and throughout the world. In addition, over 1,000 groups in the United States and abroad make The Kids on the Block puppets an effective part of their community programs.

For More Information

The Kids on the Block
9385-C Gerwig Lane
Columbia, Maryland 21046
800-368-KIDS

Family Service America
11700 West Lake Park Drive
Milwaukee, WI 53224
Referrals to local family service
   agencies (Send self-addressed
   stamped envelope.)

Rainbows for All Children
1111 W. Tower Road
Schaumburg, IL 60173
312-310-1880
Peer support groups for children
   in single-parent homes

The Step Family Foundation
   National Headquarters
333 West End Avenue
New York, NY 10023
212-877-3244
Quarterly newsletter, publications,
   telephone counseling